Samuel French Acting Edition

D0546495

Dead Man's Cell Phone

by Sarah Ruhl

SAMUELFRENCH.COM   SAMUELFRENCH.CO.UK

FOR PRODUCTION ENQUIRIES

UNITED STATES AND CANADA
Info@SamuelFrench.com
1-866-598-8449

UNITED KINGDOM AND EUROPE
Plays@SamuelFrench.co.uk
020-7255-4302

Each title is subject to availability from Samuel French, depending upon country of performance. Please be aware that DEAD MAN'S CELL PHONE may not be licensed by Samuel French in your territory. Professional and amateur producers should contact the nearest Samuel French office or licensing partner to verify availability.

MUSIC USE NOTE

IMPORTANT BILLING AND CREDIT REQUIREMENTS

The world premiere production of *DEAD MANS CELL PHONE* was produced in June 2007 by Woolly Mammoth Theatre Company (Howard Shalwitz, Artistic Director) in Washington, D.C. The production was directed by Rebecca Bayla Taichman; the set design was by Neil Patel, the costume design was by Kate TurnerWalker, the lighting design was by Colin K. Bills, the sound design was by Martin Desjardins, the choreography was by Karma Camp; the properties master was Jennifer Sheetz; the dramaturg was Elissa Goetschius and the stage manager was Taryn Colberg. The cast was as follows:

A WOMAN, JEAN. . . . . Polly Noonan

A DEAD MAN, GORDON. . . . . Rick Foucheux

GORDON'S MOTHER, MRS. GOTTLIEB . . . . Sarah Marshall

GORDON'S WIDOW, HERMIA . . . . Naomi Jacobson

GORDON'S BROTHER, DWIGHT . . . . Bruce Nelson

THE OTHER WOMAN/THE STRANGER . . . . Jennifer Mendenhall

The New York premiere of *DEAD MANS CELL PHONE* was produced in March 2008 by Playwrights Horizons (Tim Sanford, Artistic Director; Leslie Marcus, Managing Director). The production was directed by Anne Bogart; the set and costume design were by G. W. Mercier, the lighting design was by Brian H Scott, the soundscape was by Darron L West and the production stage manager was Elizabeth Moreau. The cast was as follows:

A WOMAN, JEAN. . . . . Mary-Louise Parker

A DEAD MAN, GORDON. . . . . T. Ryder Smith

GORDON'S MOTHER, MRS. GOTTLIEB . . . . Kathleen Chalfant

GORDON'S WIDOW, HERMIA . . . . Kelly Maurer

GORDON'S BROTHER, DWIGHT . . . . David Aaron Baker

THE OTHER WOMAN/THE STRANGER . . . . Carla Harting

DEAD MANS CELL PHONE was produced in March 2008 by Steppenwolf Theatre Company (Martha Lavey, Artistic Director; David Hawkanson, Executive Director). The production was directed by Jessica Thebus; the set design was by Scott Bradley, the costume design was by Linda Roethke, the lighting design was by James F. Ingalls, the sound design and original music were by Andre Pluess, the choreography was by Ann Boyd, the fight choreography was by Joe Dempsey and the stage manager was Christine D. Freeburg. The cast was as follows:

A WOMAN, JEAN . . . . Polly Noonan

A DEAD MAN, GORDON . . . . Marc Grapey

GORDON'S MOTHER, MRS. GOTTLIEB . . . . Molly Regan/
Marilyn Dodds Frank

GORDON'S WIDOW, HERMIA . . . . Mary Beth Fisher

GORDON'S BROTHER, DWIGHT . . . . Coburn Goss

THE OTHER WOMAN/THE STRANGER . . . . Sarah Charipar

ENSEMBLE . . . . Geraldine Dulex, Ben Whiting

CHARACTERS

1) a woman, Jean
2) a dead man, Gordon
3) Gordon's mother, Mrs. Gottlieb
4) Gordon's widow, Hermia
5) Gordon's brother, Dwight
6) the Other Woman/also plays the stranger. Has an accent.

SET

1) a moveable dining room table and chairs
2) a moveable cafe table
3) a cell phone
4) light

*One could technically double-cast the roles of Dwight/Gordon. One could also technically double cast Hermia/the other woman. Double-casting would require virtuosity on the part of the actors and a resistance to pure camp, and some good wigs. Judge for yourself the aesthetics at stake. I understand that these are dark economic times, and a four person play might be just the thing. When economic times change, add three angel-waiters to the cast, have them move the furniture, and pay them handsomely.

NOTES

A wonderful fact to reflect upon, that every human creature is constituted to be that profound secret and mystery to every other. A solemn
consideration, when I enter a great city by night, that every one of those
darkly clustered houses encloses its own secret; that every beating heart
in the hundreds of thousands of breasts there, is, in some of its imagin-
ings, a secret to the heart nearest it! Something of the awfulness, even
of Death itself, is referable to this. No more can I turn the leaves of this
dear book that I loved, and vainly hope in time to read it all.... It was
appointed that the book should shut with a spring, for ever and for ever,
when I had read but a page.... My friend is dead, my neighbour is dead,
my love, the darling of my soul, is dead... In any of the burial-places of
this city through which I pass, is there a sleeper more inscrutable than
its busy inhabitants are, in their innermost personality, to me, or than I
am to them?.... The messenger on horseback had exactly the same pos-
sessions as the King, the first Minister of State, or the richest merchant
in London. So with the three passengers shut up in the narrow compass
of one lumbering old mail-coach; they were mysteries to one another, as
complete as if each had been in his own coach and six, or his own coach
and sixty, with the breadth of a county between him and the next.
                                        – Charles Dickens, *Tale of Two Cities*

> "...you have done a braver thing
>   Than all the Worthies did;
> And a braver thence will spring,
>   Which is, to keep that hid."
>   – John Donne, *The Undertaking*

"In Hopper's paintings there is a lot of waiting going on...They are like
characters whose parts have deserted them and now, trapped in the
space of their waiting, must keep themselves company"
                                        – Mark Strand, *Hopper*

ACKNOWLEDGEMENTS:

Many thanks to Rebecca Taichman and to Howard Shalwitz for all of the love you brought to the first incarnation of this play, for putting your full faith in it, and in me. To Anne Bogart and to Tim Sanford for finding the play's second legs with such beautiful insight. And to Jessica Thebus and Martha Lavey for understanding that a play needs a third production to finish the thing – and to Jessica for reading the first, second, third... twelfth drafts, of this play, and all the others. To the extraordinary actors who helped me crack this play – to Mary-Louise, forever Z; to Polly, the conscience of the play; to Bill for finding Gordon before he had to leave, to T. for memorizing twelve pages in two days, to Kathleen for the divine spark, and to David, Carla, Kelly, the WADS, Sarah, Jennifer, Naomi, Rick for being so open to fabulation. Thanks to all the designers, and to Scott for the open mouth and paper houses. This play was written with the support of the Djerassi foundation, was commissioned by Sonya Sobieski and Tim Sanford at Playwrights' Horizons, and had a reading at the Lark and at New Dramatists early on its life. Thanks to Annie Cheney for her book *Body Brokers*. Thanks to the woman who worked at the Holocaust Museum who returned my cell phone to me. Oh, and thanks to the cowboy who sold me my first cell phone at the base of a mountain in a far off land.

for anthony
first braid:
two parts, now three.

Scene One

An almost empty cafe.
A dead man, Gordon,
sits on a chair with his back to us.
He doesn't look all that dead.
He looks – still.
At another table, a woman – Jean –
sits, drinking coffee, and writing a thank-you letter.
She has an insular quality,
as though she doesn't want to take up space.
She looks over at the man.
She stares back at her coffee.
She sips.
A cell phone rings.
It is coming from the dead man's table.
It rings and rings.
The caller hangs up and calls again.
Jean looks over at him.
She sighs.
The phone keeps ringing.

JEAN. Excuse me – are you going to get that?

No answer from the man.

Would you mind answering your phone?

JEAN. I'm sorry to bother you.
If you could just – turn your phone – *off?*

The cell phone rings again.
Jean gets out of her chair and walks over to the man.

JEAN. Are you ill?

No answer.

JEAN. Are you deaf?

No answer.

11

JEAN. Oh, I'm sorry –

Jean signs in sign language:

Are you deaf?

No response.
The phone rings again.

JEAN. All right.
Excuse me.

She reaches for the cell phone. She answers it.

JEAN. Hello? No. This is – you don't know me.

To the dead man:

Are you Gordon?

No answer.

I don't know. Can I take a message?
Hold on – I don't have anything to write with.

She sees a pen on the dead man's table.

To the dead man:

Thank you.

To the phone:

Go ahead.

She writes on a napkin.

How late can he call you?

The voice on the phone begins to sob.

I'm sorry. You sound upset. I'm not –

The caller hangs up.

Gordon?

She touches his shoulder.

Oh –

*She checks with a spoon under his nose to
see if he's still breathing.*

The phone rings again.
She answers it.

Hello? No, he's not. Can I take a message?

*A pause as the person on the other end
makes a very long offer.*

No, he doesn't want one. He already has one.

No, I don't want one.

I already have one.

Thank you, good-bye.

*She hangs up.
She looks around for help.*

Help.

She dials 911.

Hello?

I think that there is a dead man sitting next to me.

I don't know how he died.

I'm at a cafe.

I don't know.

Hold on.

*She exits with the cell phone to look at the name of the
cafe and the address.
We just see the dead man and an empty stage.
She returns.*

JEAN. It's on the corner of Green and Goethe. *(pronounced
  Go-thee)*

Should I stay with him?

There seems to be no one working at this cafe.

How long?

Thank you.

*She hangs up.
A pause.
She looks at him.
His cell phone rings again.*

Hello? No, he's not.

I'm – answering his phone.

Does he have your phone number?

Pause while the woman on the phone says:
of course he has my phone number. I am his mother.
The enormity of her loss registers for Jean.

Oh…Yes, of course.

He'll – I'll leave him the message.

Have a – hope you have a – good day.

Good-bye.

She hangs up.
She breathes, to Gordon.

JEAN. It was your mother.

She looks at Gordon's face.
It is transfigured, as though he was just looking at
something he found eminently beautiful.
She touches his forehead.

JEAN. Do you want me to keep talking until they get here?

Gordon, I'm Jean.

You don't know me.

But you're going to be just fine.

Well, actually –

Don't worry.

Are you still inside there?

How did you die so quietly?

I'll stay with you.

Gordon.

For as long as you need me.

I'll stay with you.

Gordon.

She holds his hand.
She keeps hold of it.
The sound of sirens, rain, and church.

Scene Two

A church.
A Mass is being sung in Latin.
Jean kneels down, wearing a dark blue rain-coat.
Her cell phone rings.
She looks at it.
She hesitates.
She answers it.
She whispers.

JEAN. Hello?

No, he can't come to the phone right now.

On the line, inaudible to us, a woman says:
I know he's dead.

Oh, you do?

I'm sorry.

Then – why?

Okay, I'll meet you.

What will you be wearing?

A pause while the woman says:
I will be wearing a blue rain coat.

Really? That's strange.

I'll be wearing a blue rain-coat too.

I'll see you then. Good-bye.

Mass continues to be sung.
Jean kneels. She prays.
A spot-light on Jean.

JEAN. Help me, God.

Help me to comfort his loved ones.

Help me to help the memory of Gordon

live on in the minds and hearts of his loved ones.

I only knew him for a short time, God.

But I think that I loved him, in a way.

Dear God. I hope that Gordon is peaceful now.

The music stops.
A woman comes to a podium.
Mrs. Gottlieb begins her eulogy.

MRS. GOTTLIEB. I'm not sure what to say. There is, thank God, a vaulted ceiling here. I am relieved to find that there is stained glass and the sensation of height. Even though I am not a religious woman I am glad there are still churches. Thank God there are still people who build churches for the rest of us so that when someone dies – or gets married – we have a place to —. I could not put all of this – *(she thinks the word grief)* – in a low-ceilinged room – no – it requires height.

A cell phone rings in the back of the church. Jean turns to look.

Could some one please turn their fucking cell phone off. There are only one or two sacred places left in the world today. Where there is no ringing. The theater, the church, and the toilet. But some people actually answer their phones in the shitter these days. Some people really do so. How many of you do? Raise your hand if you've answered your cell phone while you were quietly urinating. Yes, I thought so. My God.

Where was I? A reading from Charles' Dickens' *Tale of Two Cities.* "A wonderful fact to reflect upon, that every human creature is constituted to be that profound secret and mystery to every other. No more can I turn the leaves of this dear book…than the book should shut, forever, when I had read but a page…My friend is dead, my neighbour is dead, my love, the darling of my soul –

Jean's cell phone rings. She fumbles for it and shuts it off. Mrs. Gottlieb looks up and sees the audience.
Well.

Look at this great big sea of people wearing dark colors. It used to be you saw someone wearing black and you knew their beloved had died. Now everyone wears black all the time. We are in a state of perpetual mourning. But for what.

Where was I? Gordon.

Well. I've forgotten my point. Let's have a hymn.
Father?

A hymn.
Preferably "You'll never walk alone."
The singing begins.
Jean's cell phone rings.
Jean sneaks out, covering the phone.

You'll never walk alone. That's right. Because you'll
always have a machine in your pants that might ring.
Oh, Gordon.

She sings too.

Scene Three

A cafe.
Film noir music.
The Other Woman waiting in a blue rain-coat.
Jean enters in a blue rain-coat.

JEAN. Hello.

OTHER WOMAN. Hello.

Thank you for meeting me.

JEAN. Not at all.

OTHER WOMAN. We like the same clothes.

JEAN. Yes.

OTHER WOMAN. I suppose that's not surprising, given the circumstances.

JEAN. I don't know what you mean.

OTHER WOMAN. You don't need to pretend.

JEAN. I know.

OTHER WOMAN. Gordon has good taste. You're pretty.

JEAN. I'm not –

OTHER WOMAN. Don't be modest. I like it when a woman knows she's beautiful. Women nowadays – they don't know how to walk into a room. A beautiful woman should walk into a room thinking: I am beautiful and I know how to walk in these shoes. There's so little glamour in the world these days. It makes daily life such a bore. Women are responsible for enlivening dull places like train stations. There is hardly any pleasure in waiting for a train anymore. The women just – walk in. Horrible shoes. No confidence. Bad posture.

She looks at Jean's posture.
Jean sits up straighter.

OTHER WOMAN. A woman should be able to take out her compact and put lipstick on her lips with absolute confidence. No apology.

The other woman takes out lipstick
and puts it on her lips, slowly.
Jean is riveted.

JEAN. I've always been embarrassed to put lipstick on in public.

OTHER WOMAN. That's crap. Here – You have beautiful lips.

She hands Jean the lipstick.

JEAN. No – that's –

OTHER WOMAN. I don't have a cold.

JEAN. It's not the germs. It's –

OTHER WOMAN. Put it on. Take your time. Enjoy yourself.

Jean puts on some lipstick.

OTHER WOMAN. That was disappointing. Oh, well.

JEAN. I'm very sorry about Gordon. You must be – his friend?

OTHER WOMAN. Gordon didn't tell you much, did he?

JEAN. No.

OTHER WOMAN. Gordon could be quiet.

JEAN. Yes. He was quiet.

OTHER WOMAN. He must have respected you. He was quiet with women he respected. Otherwise he had a very loud laugh. Haw, haw, haw! You could hear him a mile away.

She remembers Gordon.

You must wonder why I wanted to meet with you.

JEAN. Yes.

OTHER WOMAN. You were with Gordon the day he died.

JEAN. Yes.

OTHER WOMAN. Gordon and I – we were – well –
You know. *(She thinks the word – lovers)*
And so – I wanted to know…
this is going to sound sentimental…
I wanted to know his last words.

JEAN. That's not sentimental.

OTHER WOMAN. I hate sentiment.

JEAN. I don't think that's sentimental. Really, I don't.

OTHER WOMAN. So. His last words.

JEAN. Gordon mentioned you before he died. Well, he more than mentioned you. He said: tell her that I love her. And then he turned his face away and died.

OTHER WOMAN. He said that he loved me.

JEAN. Yes.

OTHER WOMAN. I waited for such a long time.

And the words – delivered through another woman. What a shit.

The other woman looks away.
She wipes a tear away.

JEAN. It's not like that. Gordon said that he had loved many women in his life, but when he met you, everything changed. He said that other women seemed like clocks compared to you – other women just – measured time – broke the day up – but that you – you stopped time. He said you – stopped time – just by walking into a room.

OTHER WOMAN. He said that?

JEAN. Yes.

OTHER WOMAN. Oh, Gordon.

The phone rings.
Jean hesitates to answer it.

OTHER WOMAN. Aren't you going to get that?

JEAN. Yes.

She answers the phone.

JEAN. Hello?

On the other end: who is this?

My name is Jean.

Yes, of course.

How do I get there?

A pause while the mother gives directions.

JEAN. *(to the Other Woman, whispering)* Sorry.

The Other Woman shrugs her shoulders.

JEAN. All right, I'll see you then.
   Good-bye.

   Jean hangs up.

OTHER WOMAN. Who was it?

JEAN. His mother.

OTHER WOMAN. Oh, God.
   Mrs. Gottlieb?
   Let me touch up your lipstick before you go.

   She does. Jean puckers.

OTHER WOMAN. Good girl.

Scene Four

Jean and Gordon's mother, Mrs. Gottlieb,
at Mrs. Gottlieb's house.
The house smells of dry cracked curtains
that were once rich velvet.
Mrs. Gottlieb wears fur, indoors.

MRS. GOTTLIEB. I don't know why I didn't see you at the funeral.

JEAN. I was in the back.

MRS. GOTTLIEB. Would you say that you tend to blend in with a crowd?

JEAN. I don't know –

MRS. GOTTLIEB. You might wear brighter clothing. Or a little mascara.

JEAN. It was a funeral, so I wore black.

MRS. GOTTLIEB. Fine, fine. That's beside the point.
Gordon left his telephone to you?

JEAN. Yes – he left it to me.

MRS. GOTTLIEB. Why?

JEAN. He wanted me to have it.
Why did you call him on the phone – *after* the funeral?

MRS. GOTTLIEB. I call him everyday.
I keep forgetting that he's dead.
I do a little errand, take out my purse, and call Gordon while I'm stopped in traffic.
It's habit.

JEAN. I'm very sorry. It must be awful to lose a child.

MRS. GOTTLIEB. It is. When someone older than you dies it gets better every day but when someone younger than you dies it gets worse every day. Like grieving in reverse.

JEAN. I'm so sorry.

MRS. GOTTLIEB. I see it as my job to mourn him until the day I die.

JEAN. Oh – yes…

MRS. GOTTLIEB. Please, sit down.

Jean sits down.

MRS. GOTTLIEB. So.

JEAN. So.

MRS. GOTTLIEB. Does anyone continue to call Gordon?

JEAN. Yes.

MRS. GOTTLIEB. Who?

JEAN. Some business acquaintances who don't know that he's dead.

MRS. GOTTLIEB. And do you tell them he's – (*she thinks the word dead?*)

JEAN. Yes.

MRS. GOTTLIEB. I can't bring myself to tell anyone.

JEAN. I understand.

MRS. GOTTLIEB. It's so painful, you have no idea.

| **JEAN.** (*overlapping*) | **MRS. GOTTLIEB.** |
| No, I don't. | What it's like to lose a child. |

JEAN. No.

MRS. GOTTLIEB. You don't have children?

JEAN. No.

MRS. GOTTLIEB. Why not?

JEAN. I might have them, one day.

MRS. GOTTLIEB. You're getting older. How old are you?

JEAN. Almost forty.

MRS. GOTTLIEB. Married?

JEAN. No.

MRS. GOTTLIEB. How do you expect to have children then?

JEAN. I don't know. I could –

MRS. GOTTLIEB. When you're thirty-nine your eggs are actually forty, you know.

JEAN. I could adopt.

MRS. GOTTLIEB. It's better to have your own. They resemble

– it's the little ticks – the family eyebrow – Gordon's
eyebrow –

She makes a little line in the air,
indicating his eyebrow shape.
The mother tries not to cry.

JEAN. I'm sorry.

MRS. GOTTLIEB. Gordon – and I – had a falling out – you
know – after that, he never returned my phone calls –

JEAN. He called you the day he died.

MRS. GOTTLIEB. What? How do you know?

JEAN. Your number was on the out-going calls.

MRS. GOTTLIEB. It was?

JEAN. Yes. It said: Mom.

MRS. GOTTLIEB. Let me see.

JEAN. I deleted it by mistake.

MRS. GOTTLIEB. Gordon called me.

JEAN. Yes.

MRS. GOTTLIEB. He wanted to speak with me.

JEAN. Yes.

MRS. GOTTLIEB. How did you know Gordon, anyway?

JEAN. We worked together.

MRS. GOTTLIEB. Really.

JEAN. Yes.

MRS. GOTTLIEB. No wonder you don't have children.

JEAN. What do you mean?

MOTHER. Gordon's line of work was – toxic.

JEAN. It could be.

MRS. GOTTLIEB. Did you do the out-going or the in-coming
business?

JEAN. In-coming.

MRS. GOTTLIEB. Oh – I see.

Why don't you stay for dinner. Gordon's brother will
be here. And Gordon's wife – you know – his widow.

JEAN. Oh, I wouldn't want to intrude. You must need family
time now.

MRS. GOTTLIEB. You knew my son. I insist that you stay.

JEAN. If it would help.

MRS. GOTTLIEB. Yes, I think it would. You're very comforting, I don't know why. You're like a very small casserole – has anyone ever told you that?

JEAN. No.

MRS. GOTTLIEB. Are you religious?

JEAN. A little.

MRS. GOTTLIEB. I see. We're not religious. Our name means God-loving in German but we're not German anymore. Hermia chose a Catholic mass for Gordon because she likes to kneel and get up. I did not raise my children with any religion. Perhaps I should have. Certain brands of guilt can be inculcated in a secular way but other brands of guilt can only be obtained with reference to the metaphysical. Gordon did not experience enough guilt. Dinner will be served at seven. Do you eat meat?

JEAN. Um – Kind of.

MRS. GOTTLIEB. Good. We'll be having large quantities of meat. I'm a little anemic, you know. I eat a large steak every day and it just goes right through me.

JEAN. Oh, I'm sorry.

MRS. GOTTLIEB. So – seven o'clock.

JEAN. Seven o'clock. Great. I'm just going to run out for a moment – I have an errand –

MRS. GOTTLIEB. Very good, Jean. We'll see you at seven.

Scene Five

Gordon's brother, Dwight.
Gordon's widow, Hermia.
Gordon's Mother.
And Jean.
Everyone wears black, except for the mother, who is in a bright red get up.
A flurry of activity getting to the table.
Everyone sits in the wrong spot.

MRS. GOTTLIEB. Place cards, there are place cards!

Everyone moves to their assigned place,
saying things like:
Oh, oh, sorry, excuse me.

Jean stares at Dwight.
He looks so much like Gordon.
But Jean doesn't want to
remind anyone of Gordon's death,
so she doesn't comment on the resemblance.
A silence.

HERMIA. Gordon used to sit – there.

She points to Jean.

DWIGHT. That's right, he did.

JEAN. Oh, I'll move –

MRS. GOTTLIEB. No, no, time to move on, no time like the present.

They all look at Jean for a long moment.
Jean hiccups.

JEAN. Excuse me, I'm sorry. I have the hiccups.

Jean stands up and hiccups.

MRS. GOTTLIEB. There's water through there, dear.

JEAN. Thanks.

Jean exits and hiccups.

HERMIA. What a strange duck.

MRS. GOTTLIEB. Yes, but she knew Gordon. Try to be welcoming, Hermia.

DWIGHT. How'd she know Gordon?

MRS. GOTTLIEB. Work.

The mother nods knowingly.
Everyone murmurs knowingly
and says things like:
Really? You don't say. Well...Mmm. Hmm...

DWIGHT. Out-going?

MRS. GOTTLIEB. In-coming.

Or so she says.

They murmur knowingly.
Jean enters.
A silence.
She sits down.
She hiccups.

JEAN. Oh! Excuse me. My hiccups are so loud.

MRS. GOTTLIEB. Yes, they are, aren't they? Remarkably loud hiccups for such a small woman.

DWIGHT. Mother. Come with me, Jean. I'll show you my secret. It's drinking a glass of bourbon upsidown.

JEAN. Okay. *(hiccup)* Thank you.

Dwight pulls Jean's chair out for her.
Jean and Dwight exit to the kitchen.

HERMIA. Dwight likes her.

MRS. GOTTLIEB. I thought he might.

A silence.

HERMIA. Are you sad?

MRS. GOTTLIEB. Yes, are you?

HERMIA. Yes. So sad that it's – awful. Now I know why they call it awful sad.

MRS. GOTTLIEB. I'm glad we can share this, Hermia. We loved him most of all.

HERMIA. I hope that – the two of us – can continue to – mourn together – Mrs. Gottlieb. I feel so all alone sometimes.

MRS. GOTTLIEB. Call me Harriet.

HERMIA. Harriet.

MOTHER. I never could get used to Gordon having a wife but now that he's dead you're going to be a very great comfort to me, Hermia.

It is one of the first nice things Mrs. Gottlieb has ever said to her.
Jean and Dwight re-enter.
Jean is laughing.

DWIGHT. That's better.

JEAN. Dwight got rid of my hiccups!

MRS. GOTTLIEB. You're amazing, Dwight. You have so many hidden talents. Always have. Remember when Dwight was little and he could grow stiff as a board and his friends pretended he was a plank or a dead insect and they would carry him around the living room at my lunch parties and how we all would laugh! Oh. I guess there's no one here to remember that.

A silence.

MRS. GOTTLIEB. Well. Let's eat. Rib-eye steak. Do you like rib-eye, Jean? Nothing better in the world, I tell you. Ribbons of flesh, ribbons of fat, all in one bite. Dwight, why don't you carve.

Dwight takes up the carving knife.
He's never carved before. It was Gordon's job.

JEAN. Um –

MRS. GOTTLIEB. A hiccup?

JEAN. No, I'm –

DWIGHT. She's talking, mother.

MRS. GOTTLIEB. Oh.

JEAN. I brought some presents for all of you. From Gordon.

DWIGHT. You did?

JEAN. Yes. In his last moments. He wanted to give each of you something. From the café. Before he died. He was thinking of all of you.

Dwight puts down the carving knife.
Jean gets out a little bag of presents.

JEAN. This salt is for you, Hermia. Because he said you were the salt of the earth.

Hermia takes the salt-shaker.
She is moved.

HERMIA. Thank you.

JEAN. And this is for you, Dwight.

Jean gives Dwight a cup.

JEAN. Because Gordon said you were like – a cup. Because you can hold things. Beautiful things. And they don't – pour out.

Dwight is moved.
He takes the cup.

DWIGHT. Gordon said that?

JEAN. Yes.

DWIGHT. Wow.

JEAN. And this is for you, Harriet.

She gives Gordon's mother a spoon.

JEAN. Because of your cooking.

There is a silence.
Everyone is still.

MRS. GOTTLIEB. What did he mean by that?

JEAN. I – when he was little – and grew up – eating – your food –

MRS. GOTTLIEB. No –

JEAN. It was only a nice – he meant it nicely.

MRS. GOTTLIEB. HE COULD NOT HAVE MEANT THAT NICELY!

Mrs. Gottlieb slams down her chair and exits.
Dwight goes after her.

DWIGHT. Excuse me.

Dwight exits.

JEAN. What did I – ?

HERMIA. We never talk about her cooking.

JEAN. I'm so sorry.

HERMIA. Don't worry. She's just – you know.

Hermia plays with her salt.

HERMIA. I love the salt.

Hermia is sad.

HERMIA. Did he use any of it? On his food?

JEAN. Yes, he sprinkled it on his potatoes before he died.

HERMIA. Oh…how beautiful…His last flavor. Oh.

JEAN. I'm glad you like it.

HERMIA. Yes, I do.

You know, I always thought if Gordon died I'd never want to see my in-laws ever again, and I'd be happy and relieved to never lay eyes on them again, but now that Gordon's dead they sort of remind me of him, and it sort of comforts me. You know?

The mother enters.

MRS. GOTTLIEB. *(to Jean)* I'm going to have to ask you to leave.

DWIGHT. We haven't even cut the meat, mother. Jean hasn't eaten –

MRS. GOTTLIEB. All right, Dwight. You seem to know what's best for the household. Why don't you take over now that Gordon's dead. I know that's what you've always wanted. *(with a nasty look at Dwight.)*

I'm going to lie down. Upstairs. Hermia – come with me. You can put a cold compress on my head. Dwight – be sure she *eats* something. I'm afraid if she doesn't eat she'll disappear into the *ether.* Poof.

Mrs. Gottlieb and Hermia exit.

DWIGHT. Can I cut you some meat?

JEAN. I'm sort of a vegetarian.

DWIGHT. Oh – I'm so sorry. Why didn't you say so?

JEAN. I didn't want to impose. I think people should be polite when someone cooks a meal for them. Even semi-vegetarians. I mean a foolish consistency is a hobgoblin of little minds. Isn't it?

DWIGHT. I've always thought so.

They look around at the table.

Well – it looks like there's only meat.

JEAN. That's okay.

DWIGHT. Let me look in the kitchen. Hold on.

Dwight exits.
Jean sits alone.
She looks small and tired.
An Edward Hopper painting, for 5 seconds.
Dwight re-enters with some caramel popcorn.

DWIGHT. How about some caramel popcorn?

JEAN. Okay.

DWIGHT. I'm sorry about my mother.
She can be a little –

JEAN. She must be in a state of shock.

DWIGHT. I guess. She's always got – a little shock – to her.

JEAN. I'm sure she's a nice person, deep down.

DWIGHT. You think so?

JEAN. I think people are usually nice, deep down, when they're put in the right circumstance. She just must be in the wrong circumstance. A lot. Or something.

DWIGHT. Yeah.

They eat some more caramel popcorn.

DWIGHT. You know why my mother named me Dwight?

JEAN. Nope.

DWIGHT. After the president you might think.

JEAN. Oh. Right. Dwight!

DWIGHT. But it's not. It's because my mother felt sorry for the name. She *felt sorry for the name Dwight*. She thought it was ignored, pushed aside. So she named me it. Can you imagine how that would affect a child?

JEAN. Did you feel pushed aside?

DWIGHT. Gordon was the mover and shaker. I always sat back a little.

JEAN. What exactly did Gordon do?

DWIGHT. You don't know?

JEAN. I –

DWIGHT. Even the people at in-coming didn't know?

JEAN. I was low on the totem pole.

DWIGHT. You still working there?

JEAN. No. As soon as Gordon died I wrote a letter of resignation.

DWIGHT. That's good. There's not much to that outfit without Gordon at the helm.

JEAN. No. He was a good boss.

DWIGHT. Mmm. So – what are you gonna do now – for a job?

JEAN. Go back to my old job, I guess.

DWIGHT. What's that?

JEAN. I work at the Holocaust museum. In the office.

DWIGHT. That's a sad job.

JEAN. It is a sad job.
      But it's good – you know – to remember.

DWIGHT. I can see that. To remember.

They eat some caramel popcorn.

DWIGHT. You like to remember stuff, don't you?

JEAN. Yeah. Why?

DWIGHT. I can tell. You're a little sentimental. It's nice. You don't see that much anymore. No one wants to remember anything.

JEAN. I want to remember everything. Even other people's memories.

DWIGHT. These digital cameras – you know – and all the digital – stuff – the informational *bits* – flying through the air – no one wants to remember. People say I love you – on cell phones – and where does it go? No paper. Remembering requires paper.

JEAN. Yeah. But maybe the air remembers. Sometimes.

DWIGHT. I hope the air remembers. But I doubt it. I like real things. I like paper. I work at a stationery store.

JEAN. Really? I *love* stationery. Do you do the monograms? And the embossed invitations?

DWIGHT. We do.

JEAN. I love those! When you touch the invitations, it feels so nice. Creamy, and thick, and you can close your eyes and *feel* the words. I think heaven must be like an embossed invitation.

DWIGHT. Yes. Creamy, and flat and deep. Like skin. Or – heaven, you were saying about heaven.

JEAN. I've never sent out an embossed invitation. But I'd like to. One day.

Dwight is proud and happy.
Jean is embarrassed for revealing too much.
They both put their hands in the caramel popcorn at the same time and realize there's none left.

DWIGHT. Well, we're out of caramel popcorn.
    Are you still hungry?

JEAN. A little.

DWIGHT. Let's go out and get us something to eat. Some vegetables.

JEAN. I'd like that.

DWIGHT. You like broccoli? Or zucchini?

JEAN. Sure.

DWIGHT. Which one.

JEAN. Both.

DWIGHT. Great. We'll get some at the grocery store. Then maybe you could come see the stationery store. It's closed now, but I have the key.

JEAN. Okay.

DWIGHT. Mother! We're going out! MRS. GOTTLIEB! She's ignoring me. She'll be fine.

A strange unidentifiable sound from far away, like a door creaking, or a small animal in pain.

JEAN. What's that?

DWIGHT. It's mother crying.

JEAN. It doesn't sound like crying.

DWIGHT. She does it different. Let's go.

Scene Six

At the stationery store.
The supply closet.
The light is dim.
Jean and Dwight are touching embossed invitations,
closing their eyes.

JEAN. Feel this one. Like a leaf.

Dwight feels it.

JEAN. This one. Branches. Tablecloths. Wool.

She passes it to Dwight.

JEAN. This one is my favorite one, though. I'd like to live in a little house made of this one.

She passes it to Dwight .

DWIGHT. A house made of paper.

Dwight tries to build a little house out of the paper.

JEAN. Yeah.
And this one! Braided hair.

Dwight touches it.

DWIGHT. Can I braid your hair?
JEAN. What?
Okay.

Dwight stands behind Jean and fumbles with her hair.

DWIGHT. Am I pulling too hard?
JEAN. No, that's fine. It feels nice.

A pause while Dwight braids her hair.

JEAN. You know what's funny? I never had a cell phone. I didn't want to always *be there*, you know. Like if your phone is on you're supposed to be there. Sometimes I like to disappear. But it's like – when everyone has their cell phone on, no one is there. It's like we're all disappearing the more we're there. Last week there was this woman in line at the pharmacy and she was like, "Shit, Shit!" on her cell phone and she kept saying "shit, fuck, you're shitting me, you're fucking shitting me, no fucking way, bitch, if you're shitting me I'll fucking kill you" you know, that kind of thing, and there were all these old people in line and it was like she didn't care if she told her whole life, the worst part of her life, in front of the people in line. It was like – people who are in line at pharmacies must be strangers. By definition. And I thought that was sad.

But when Gordon's phone rang and rang, after he died, I thought his phone was beautiful, like it was the only thing keeping him alive, like as long as people called him he would be alive. That sounds – a little – I know – but all those molecules, in the air, trying to talk to Gordon – and Gordon – he's in the air too – so maybe they all would meet up there, whizzing around – those bits of air – and voices.

DWIGHT. I wonder how long it will take before no one calls him again and then he will be truly gone.

JEAN. I wonder too. I'll leave his phone on as long as I live. I'll keep re-charging it. Just in case someone calls. Maybe an old childhood friend. You never know.

DWIGHT. Did you love my brother?

JEAN. I didn't know him well enough to love him.

DWIGHT. It kind of seems like you do.

JEAN. Were the two of you very close?

DWIGHT. We had our moments. Gordon wasn't always – easy.

JEAN. Tell me a story about him.

DWIGHT. One time Gordon made up a character named Mr. Big X and he said: I'll take you to meet Mr. Big X! I was really excited to meet Mr. Big X. But in order to meet him, Gordon wrapped me up in a blanket and pushed me down the stairs.

JEAN. You have any nice stories about Gordon?

DWIGHT. Yeah. They're just harder to remember, you know. No imprint. Like – one time we had dinner and – Gordon was nice to me – and – what kind of story is that...

JEAN. You crying?

DWIGHT. I'm okay.

JEAN. How's that braid coming?

DWIGHT. It's pretty good. I've never done a braid before.

Jean reaches up and feels the braid.

JEAN. It's good. Only you did two parts, not three.

DWIGHT. Huh?

JEAN. Usually a braid has three parts. Two parts is more like a twist. But that's fine. I bet it's pretty from the back.

DWIGHT. It does look pretty.

Here – let me show you –

He tries to show her the twist.
Their faces are close to each other,
in the dark, in the back of the stationery store.
Jean and Dwight kiss.
Gordon's cell phone rings.

DWIGHT. Don't answer that.

JEAN. It could be –

DWIGHT. Don't get it. It'll take a message, okay?

JEAN. But I can't get Gordon's messages – I don't have his password! I'll never know who called –

DWIGHT. *(overlapping)* Their number – on the in-coming calls – will be saved.

Okay?

JEAN. Okay.

The phone rings.
They kiss.
Embossed stationery moves through the air slowly,
like a snow parade.
Lanterns made of embossed paper,
houses made of embossed paper,
light falling on paper,
falling on Jean and Dwight,
who are also falling.

Gordon walks on stage.
He opens his mouth, as if to speak to the audience.
Black-out.

Intermission

PART TWO

Scene One:
the last day of gordon's life

GORDON, *to the audience:*

GORDON. I woke up that morning – the day I died – thinking I'd like a lobster bisque.

I showered. I had breakfast. Hermia has it timed so she finishes her cereal just as I begin mine. Something proud and untouchable about the way she eats her shredded wheat. A rebuke in the rhythm of her chewing, the curve of her back as she finishes her last bite, standing, washing out the bowl. Who cleans the bowl while they're chewing the last bite? She washes the bowl like this. Getting rid of all the unchewed bits. No respect for the discarded.

I ran to the subway in the rain. I didn't say good-bye. I didn't have an umbrella. I thought about going back for an umbrella, maybe giving Hermia an old fashioned kiss on the cheek that would soften her face, but I remembered the curve of her implacable back and I forged ahead in the rain, umbrella-less.

You know when people are so crushed together in the rain, in the city, so many people, that no one person needs an umbrella, because one umbrella covers three bodies. And everyone's yelling into their cell phones, and I'm thinking: where have all the phone booths gone? The phone booths are all dead. People are yammering into their phones and I hear fragments of lost love and hepatitis and I'm thinking, is there no privacy? *Is there no dignity?*

I get onto the subway. A tomb for people's eyes. I believe that when people are in transit their souls are not in their bodies. It takes a couple minutes to catch up. Walking

– horseback – that is the speed at which the soul can stay in the body during travel. So airports and subway stations are very similar to hell. People are vulnerable – disembodied – they're looking around for their souls while they get a shoe shine. That's when you bomb them. In transit. But I didn't know that then. I was on the subway buried in some advertisement for a dermatology office, thinking about the sale of a cornea. The way I'm talking now – this is hind-sight. My mind went: dermatology – cornea – rain – umbrella – Hermia's a bitch – lobster bisque.

I wouldn't really say that I sell organs for a living. I connect people – see: A man in Iran needs money real bad but he doesn't need his own kidney. A woman in Sydney needs a new kidney but she doesn't need her own cash.

I put these two together. You're a sick person, you want to deal with red tape? You want to be put on hold – listen to bad music on the phone for seven years while you wait for your organs to dry out – is that love? No. Is that compassion? No. I make people feel good about their new organs. I call it: compassionate obfuscation. There are parts enough to make everyone whole; it's just that the right parts are not yet in the right bodies. We need the right man to – redistribute. One umbrella covers three bodies.

Truth for its own sake – I've never understood the concept. Morality can be measured by results: how good do you make people feel? You make them feel good? Then you're a good man. You make people live longer? Great. Is it my job to stop executions in China? I don't have that power. What I *can* do, however, is make sure that these miserable fucks who die for no good reason *have* a reason – I make sure their organs go to someone who needs them.

There was this surgeon I knew who did organ extractions in China – a highly trained surgeon – he couldn't stand it after a while – political prisoners, not even dead yet, made him sick. Now he's a sushi chef in New Jersey. I showed up one day at his counter. I ate his hamachi – excellent. I don't dip my sashimi in soy sauce. Sushi is for adults. You want to really taste your sushi, taste it. Don't drown it in soy sauce, that's for children. I

enjoyed my food in silence. I thanked him in Chinese.
He looked a little startled. People assume he's Japanese. I said to him in Mandarin: you don't want people
to know about your old line of work, neither do I. Left
it at that. Ate my sushi. You can tell with tuna whether
they slice it from the belly or from the tail end. He
always gave me the belly. It's the good part.

But that day – the day I died – I didn't want to eat
something that reminded me of body parts. I woke
up in the morning wanting a lobster bisque. So I get
off the subway, go to the cafe, the place I always go.
A familiar guy behind the counter, a giant, with really
huge knuckles. I said, I'll have the lobster bisque. He
said, sorry we're out, as though it was a casual, everyday thing to be out of lobster bisque on the day I was
going to die, as though I could come back the following week. As though it were a friendly, careless matter
– sorry, we're out.

So I said: did you have any ten minutes ago?
And the giant said, yes.
I said, is anyone at this restaurant currently eating a
lobster bisque?
And the giant said, well yes.
Who?
And he pointed to a woman in the corner. A pale-ish
woman, sort of non-descript.
So I say, I will purchase her bowl of soup.
What? He says. I take out my wallet, pull out a hun-
dred.
Then I see it – she is tilting the bowl to the side to
scrape out the last bite.
I watch it go into her little mouth, slow motion.
Son of a bitch, I say. I'll have lentil.

I'm used to getting what I want. But today is not my
day. So I have the lentil.

Lentil soup is never that great. It's only ever serviceable. It doesn't really make your mouth water, does it,

lentil soup? Something watery – something brown – and hot carrots. Like death. Serviceable, a little mushy and warm in the wrong places, not as bad as you'd think it's going to be, not as good, either.

Suddenly I feel my heart – compressing – like a terrible bird in my chest. And I think – I'm finally punished. Someone is going to sell my heart to someone in Russia. Then I think – use your cell phone. Call your wife. Tell her to give you a decent burial, organs in tact. But the wife's not supposed to know you sell organs for a living. So just call the wife and say good-bye. But no – she doesn't love you enough to have the right tone of voice on your death bed. The kind of voice you'd like to hear – indescribably tender. A death-bed voice.

Gordon having a heart-attack, heaving.

No longer holding it in – the things people hold back from each other – whole lives – most people give in at the last moment – but not Hermia, no – she'll be sealed up – she'll keep a little bit extra for herself – that last nugget of pride – she'll reserve it for her tin can spine – so she'll have an extra half inch of height. That thing – that wedge, that cold wedge between – I can't call her. No. A disappointment. So call your mistress. Or mother. No – mother would say – what a way to die, Gordon, in a café? No, not mother. Dwight? A man doesn't call his brother on his death-bed – no – he wants a woman's voice – But the heart keeps on heaving itself up – out of my chest – into my mouth – and I'm thinking – that bitch over there ate all the lobster bisque, this is all her fault – and I look over at her, and she looks like an angel – not like a bitch at all – and I think – good – good – I'm glad she had the last bite – I'm glad.
Then I die.

Light on Gordon's face, transfigured.
Gordon dies again.
And Gordon disappears.

Scene Two

Jean and Dwight in a love haze
in the back of the stationery store.

DWIGHT. I was dreaming about you. And a letter press. I dreamed you were the letter z.

JEAN. Why Z?

DWIGHT. Two lines – us – connected by a diagonal. Z.

JEAN. Oh, Dwight.

DWIGHT. If we are ever parted, and can't recognize each other, because of death, or some other calamity – just say the letter Z – to me – it will be our password.

JEAN. Z.

DWIGHT. Let's never be parted. I don't need more than twelve hours to know you, Jean. Do you?
Tell me you don't. We exchanged little bits of our souls – I have a little of yours and you have a little of mine – like a torn jacket – you gave me one of your buttons.
I – I love you Jean.

The phone rings.

DWIGHT. Don't get that.

JEAN. It'll just take a second.
Hello?
Are you sitting down?

This might come as a very great shock to you.	DWIGHT. Jean? Who's on the
But Gordon has passed away.	phone?

JEAN. I'm sorry, who is this?
(to Dwight) a business colleague.
(to the phone) The funeral was yesterday.
Yes, it was a very nice service.
It was Catholic so it wasn't very personal –
I'm sorry – are you Catholic?
Oh, good – I mean –

DWIGHT. *(whispering)* Jean – come here…

> *The voice on the phone offers Jean his condolences.*

JEAN. *(to Dwight)* I'm on the phone!
(to the phone) Yes, in-coming. Thank you,
but if you want to offer condolences,
the best thing would probably be to
write to Hermia and Harriet Gottleib.
Their address is 111 Shank avenue.

DWIGHT. *(no longer whispering)* Jean!

JEAN. *(to Dwight)* I'm on the phone!
(to the phone) I don't know anything about a living will
– no –
I'm sorry. I have to go.
I hope you have a pleasant day
in spite of the bad news.
Good-bye.

> *She hangs up.*

DWIGHT. Who was that?

JEAN. A business colleague.

DWIGHT. I don't think you want to get mixed up in that.

JEAN. Oh, Dwight, I'll be all right.

DWIGHT. I forbid you to talk to Gordon's colleagues.

JEAN. You *forbid* me?

DWIGHT. Get rid of the phone. Give it up. It's bad luck.

JEAN. It brought me to you, didn't it?

DWIGHT. It's not good for you. Life is for the living. Me.
You. Living. Life, life, life!

> *The phone rings.*

DWIGHT. If you answer that phone, Jean, if you answer that
phone –

JEAN. What?

DWIGHT. I will! –
it will make me sad.

JEAN. I have to answer it, Dwight.
Sometimes it seems like you didn't even love your own
brother.

She answers it. Dwight crumples.

JEAN. Hello?
Jean speaking.
(to Dwight) It's Hermia.
She needs a ride home.

Scene Three

Hermia and Jean drinking cosmopolitans.

HERMIA. Give me another. Don't worry, I can drive home after all, Jean.

JEAN. You think so?

HERMIA. If I drive with my face. Haw haw haw! Oh, God, I sound like Gordon.

JEAN. You must have a lot on your mind. Do you want to talk?

HERMIA. Yes, in fact, I would. Lately I've been thinking of the last time I had sex with Gordon. Over the last ten years, when Gordon and I would have sex, I would pretend that I was someone else. I've heard that a lot of women, in order to come, pretend that their lover is someone else. Like a robber or Zorba the Greek or a rapist or something like that. Do you ever do that?

JEAN. No.

HERMIA. But you know what Jean? I pretended that *I* was someone else, and that Gordon was Gordon, but he was cheating on me with me – *I* was the other woman. And it would turn me on to know that Gordon's wife – me – was in the next room, that I – the mistress – had to be quiet, so that I – the wife – wouldn't hear me. You and I both know that Gordon had affairs.

JEAN. Well –

HERMIA. So the last time I had sex with Gordon I wish I could say that I wasn't pretending. That he was really in me, and I was really in him. But I was pretending to be a co-worker of Gordon's. He brought her to dinner once. That night, she was wearing a thong under a white pantsuit. (I never wear a thong. It's like having a tampon in your asshole. Don't you think?) Anyway, that last time, I imagined myself in this white pantsuit, and his hands under my thong, ripping it off. I pictured what Gordon was seeing – and I picture me, looking back at Gordon. And there is more and more desire, like two mirrors, facing each other – it's amazing what the mind can do.

After I met you, I was convinced that you and Gordon were having an affair. So after dinner, I was – you know – and I pretended to be you – and it worked. Isn't that a riot?

JEAN. That's – um –

HERMIA. I wouldn't normally tell you that but I've had a lot to drink at this point.

JEAN. You should know that I didn't have a sexual relationship with your husband.

HERMIA. Then why do you have his fucking phone?

JEAN. I was the last one with him.

HERMIA. And why was that, Jean?

JEAN. A coincidence.

HERMIA. Gordon didn't have coincidences. He had accidents. There's a difference.

The phone rings.

HERMIA. Give that to me.

She rips the phone out of Jean's hands.

HERMIA. Oops – missed the call!
Is his picture of the Pope still on it? From a business trip to Rome. Those mobs at the Vatican, waving their cell phones, stealing an image of the Pope's dead face, and Gordon among them, I can still hear him laughing, I have the Pope in my pocket. There it is. Dead Pope. Oh, I feel sick.

The phone rings again.

I'm going to bury it. Like the Egyptians.

JEAN. No.

Jean gestures for the phone. The phone keeps ringing.

HERMIA. Yes, in the ground, with Gordon. There was this Belgian man very recently in the news and the undertakers forgot to remove the cell phone from the coffin and it *rang* during the funeral! Just went on ringing! And the family is suing for negligence Jean – for *negligesh* – you have to *bury* it, see – to *bury* it – very deep so you cannot hear the sound.

48   DEAD MAN'S CELL PHONE

The phone stops ringing.

Are you ever in a very quiet room all alone and you feel as though you can hear a cell phone ringing and you look everywhere and you cannot see one but there are so many ringing in the world that you must hear some dim echo. Nothing is really silent anymore – and after a death – an almost silence – you have to bury it bury it very deep.

JEAN. I'm sorry, Hermia, but I can't let you do that. Gordon wanted me to have his phone.

Hermia hands Jean the phone.

HERMIA. Do you know what it's like marrying the wrong man, Jean? And now – now – even if he *was* the wrong man, still, he was *the* man – and I should have spent my life trying to love him instead of wishing he were someone else.

What did Charles Dickens say? That we drive alone in our separate carriages never to truly know each other and then the book shuts and then we die? Something like that?

JEAN. I don't know what Charles Dickens said.

HERMIA. What good are you, Jean. You don't even know your ass from your Dickens. Oh, God! Two separate carriages and then you die!

Hermia weeps.

JEAN. Hermia. There's something you should know. Gordon wrote you a letter before he died. There were different drafts, on napkins, all crumpled up. The waiter must have thrown them out, after the ambulance came, but I read one of the drafts.

HERMIA. What did it say?

JEAN. I forget exactly. But I can paraphrase. It said, Dear Hermia. I know we haven't always connected, every second of the day. Husbands and wives seldom do. The joy between husband and wife is elusive, but it is strong. It endures countless moments of silent betrayal, navigates complicated labyrinths of emotional retreats.

I know that sometimes you were somewhere else when we made love. I was too. But in those moments of climax, when the darkness descended, and our fantasies dissolved into the air under the quickening heat of our desire – then, *then*, we were in that room together. And that is all that matters. Love, Gordon.

HERMIA. Gordon knew that?

JEAN. I guess he did.

HERMIA. Well, how about that.

Years of her marriage come back to her with a new light shining on them.

You've given me a great gift, Jean.

JEAN. I'm glad.

HERMIA. What can I give you?

JEAN. Nothing.

HERMIA. You gave me back ten years of my marriage. You see, after I learned that Gordon's "business trips to Rome" equaled him, trafficking organs, I couldn't bring myself to –. You know – people never write into *Cosmo* about how sexual revulsion can be caused by moral revulsion – they just tell you to change positions.

JEAN. Organs?

HERMIA. Oh, yes, Gordon and his organs –
that's funny Gordon rhymes with organs, how is it I've never noticed that – - Gordon, organ/ organ, Gordon, same letters too! O, R, G – there's no D –
and God in the middle – oh! I feel sick.

JEAN. Gordon – sold organs?

HERMIA. I thought you were in in-coming.

JEAN. I was.

HERMIA. And you didn't know what was in the packages?

JEAN. No – I guess I didn't.

HERMIA. That's funny! Well, I'm sorry to ruin your illusions about Gordon. I was never supposed to know – I told my friends he was in waste management. I remember one sad case. Gordon convinced a Brazilian man to

give his kidney to a woman in Israel. Gordon paid him
five thousand dollars cash. Gordon probably made
one hundred thousand dollars in the transaction. He
bought me a yellow diamond. (I think they look like
something you'd find in a candy machine, but they're
very rare.) So the man returned to Brazil, kidneyless.
And then his money was stolen from him at the airport
in Rio. Can you imagine? He wrote these sad letters to
our home. He would draw pictures of his lost kidney.
It looked like a broken heart.

JEAN. Oh!

> *The phone rings.*
> *Jean and Hermia look at each other.*
> *Jean chooses to answer it.*

JEAN. Hello –

> *She is cut off.*
> *She listens for a while.*
> *Film noir music.*
> *She hangs up.*

JEAN. They said they have a kidney from Brazil. Go to South
Africa. To the airport. I'll be wearing a red rain-coat.
And hung up.

I have to go to South Africa.

HERMIA. What?

JEAN. I'll make up for Gordon's mistakes.

HERMIA. Too late, Jean. The kidneys, the corneas, the skin
– they're the rings on my fingers and the fixtures in
our bathrooms. What's done is done.

JEAN. Someone is *waiting* for a kidney, Hermia!
Tell Dwight I'll call him from Johannesburg.

HERMIA. What?
Jean! Do you own a gun?

> *But Jean is out the door.*

Scene Four

At the airport in Johannesburg.
Jean waits.
A stranger enters (the Other Woman who is disguised
completely and androgynously with a different accent
from the one she had before – she now has an Eastern
European accent, whereas before she had a vague, subtle,
worldly and wholly unidentifiable accent of a beautiful
woman who travels constantly between the city capitals
of Europe and South America.)
Film noir music.
The stranger wears a red raincoat and sunglasses.
The stranger takes her cell phone out
and dials a number.
Jean's cell phone rings.
She answers it.

JEAN. Hello.

STRANGER. Hello. I am right behind you.

Jean looks back at her.

STRANGER. Don't look at me.

Jean turns back.
They remain on their phones
even though they are in close proximity.

STRANGER. Place the money on the lost luggage counter.
Then hang up, and place your phone on the lost luggage, as though it is afterthought. Then check your
watch, look distracted, look up at departure screen,
and get back on a plane to your own country.

JEAN. Actually, we're in a bit of a pickle. In our country we
can only give our organs away for love. I mean I'm not
saying our country is great or anything because at the
moment – well, you know – but in terms of organ laws –
it has to be love. It's a strange law, right, because how can
you measure love? I'm not sure you *can* measure love.
In any case, if you're willing to give away your kidney
for love, then we're still in business. If not –
I am willing to give my kidney away instead of yours.

STRANGER. What?

JEAN. That's right. It was so good of you to offer. I'm sorry I have no money to give you. I did make something for you though, just a token, it's a lamp, in the shape of a kidney, it says, I was willing to give you away so that someone else shall live – so that when you turn it on –

Jean pulls out a paper mache lamp.

STRANGER. Hang up the phone. I'm coming over.

They hang up their phones.
The stranger approaches.

STRANGER. There are numbers stored on that phone. I need them.

JEAN. You can't have it.

STRANGER. I advise you to hand it over quietly.

JEAN. No, I won't. I won't!

STRANGER. Hand over the phone or I will kill you.

JEAN. That's absurd. You can't have it.

The stranger pulls out a gun.

STRANGER. You know nothing of Gordon's work, do you? It's big business. You're in over your head.

JEAN. No – I'm afraid you're in over *your* head.

Jean kicks the gun out of the stranger's hand.
Jean kicks the stranger on a special part of her leg so that she crumples to the ground.

JEAN. *(surprised at her own daring)* Whoa!

A struggle for the gun.
Perhaps an extended fight sequence
with some crawling and hair pulling.
The Stranger grabs the gun.
She points it at Jean.

STRANGER. I didn't want to have to do this, Jean, but you are forcing my hand –

The stranger hits Jean on the head with the gun.
Jean falls to the ground.
The lamp falls and breaks.
A flash of light.

Scene Five

Jean and Gordon, sitting, at a café.
As if we are at the top of the play.
You might imagine takin gestures from the very first scene
and repeating them in the following as though Jean and
Gordon are doomed to repeat their first encounter over
and over again for eternity.
Jean, sitting in front of a bowl of empty soup.
A silence.

JEAN. Do they have lobster bisque in heaven?

Jean looks up at Gordon.

GORDON. We're not in heaven. We're in a hell reserved for
people who sell organs on the black market and the
people who loved them.

JEAN. Gordon?

GORDON. That's right. When you die, you go straight to the
person you most loved, right back to the very moment,
the very place, you decided you loved them. There's a
spiritual pipeline, you might say. In life we are often
separated from what we love best – errors of timing,
of geography – but there are no errors in the afterlife.
You loved me most, Jean, so you came to me.

JEAN. What if the person you loved most didn't love you
most?

GORDON. Don't try to work it out. It's too complex. Math-
ematical hoopla. If they need three of *Jean the beloved*
why they make you into three Jeans. For the very few
it's a neat transaction – totally reciprocal. *A* loves *B*, *B*
loves *A*. However: some mothers loved their children
best, those children loved their father best, and the
father loved the family dog. Some end up with gar-
dens. The very best parents loved all their children
equally but that is rare, rare.

JEAN. How about people who loved God best?

GORDON. Don't know. Never met 'em. They go to a different laundromat.

JEAN. Laundromat?

GORDON. See you only have one costume here. Whatever you died in. So you go to the Laundromat once a week. Only you have to wash your clothes naked. It's weird – hundreds of naked people washing their socks.

JEAN. Who did you love best?

GORDON. I loved myself best of all. There's a special holding pen for us. Waiting to see if someone else will join us. Like you joined me, Jean. You're my good luck.

JEAN. But I'm not dead.

You're lying.

You lie all the live long day.

GORDON. No, *you* lie all the live long day.

All those nice lies you made up for me?

Now why did you do that, Jean?

JEAN. I saw you die. I saw your face. I wanted for you to be good.

GORDON. Aw, Jean.

JEAN. Oh, Gordon.

GORDON. You and I – we're alike. We both told lies to help other people. You decided to help a dead man because only a dead person can be 100% good. When you're alive, the goodness rubs off you if you so much as leave the house. Life is essentially a very large brillo pad.

But I digress. The point is, Jean, we're two peas in the proverbial pod. In-coming calls, out-going organs, we're all just floating receptacles – waiting to be filled – with meaning – which you and I provide. It's a talent, and I admire you.

JEAN. No – we're not alike. You made people into *parts*, into things.

Don't you feel bad about that?

GORDON. I feel done with it – that's all. Money and organs and trade – up here – it's just road kill of the mind. I'm done with organs. Didn't even donate mine. They're all in tact. I never signed that little thingy on my driver's license. Felt like a suicide note to sign it…and now…

JEAN. You don't need them.

GORDON. No.

JEAN. Take them out.

GORDON. What?

JEAN. Take them out. Put them on a cloud and lower them into South America for all the sad people who sold their own.

GORDON. Would that make you feel better, Jean? Would it?

JEAN. Yes, I think it would.

GORDON. All right, Jean.

> *Gordon puts his hand under his shirt.*
> *He tries to remove his kidney.*
> *He tries a couple of ways.*
> *He turns his back to the audience.*

GORDON. I can't get it out, Jean. I can't get it out.

Oh, I've almost got it Jean!

I can feel it coming out!

Help me get it out! It won't come out!

The skin is so tough! Uuuuugh!

> *He turns back around.*
> *His organs are still in place.*

GORDON. Couldn't do it.

JEAN. Oh God, how did I end up in your pipeline? I loved Dwight, didn't I? I don't even know you.

GORDON. You love me because I'm charismatic. I'm more charismatic than Dwight. Even dead, apparently. I spent about two seconds feeling guilty about that when I was a child, then I just went on being me. Sorry, Jean. You have to be very careful who you fall in love with, and where. A non-descript café for all time? Couldn't you have chosen better wall-hangings? Or better weather? An overcast day, for all time?

JEAN. I liked it when you couldn't talk. Could you just not talk?

Could you – pretend to be dead again? Just for a moment?

GORDON. Whatever turns you on, Jean.

He pretends to be dead.
She looks at him.
She holds his hand.
She tries to feel her old love for him.
She looks in his eyes.

JEAN. What were you looking at before you died?

GORDON. You.

JEAN. Me.

GORDON. Yes, you were eating the last bite of my soup. But I wanted you to have it. That's why my eyes looked so nice – I was giving you my last bite. They say love goes right through the eyes – bam. I saw you before I died; you didn't see me. You saw me after I died; I couldn't see you. We had star-crossed eyes. Now we can gaze and gaze for all time…

They kiss a strange kiss.

GORDON. We don't really kiss with our mouths up here. Just letting you get the hang of it.

JEAN. What do you kiss with?

GORDON. Our hair.

JEAN. Oh, God!

I am dead, aren't I?

GORDON. Yes.

JEAN. I suddenly feel very lonely.

GORDON. You can still listen to the others, you know. Invisible conversation. They're still in the air – listen:

A recording of Jean:
Should I stay with him?
There seems to be no one working at this cafe.

JEAN. You can hear cell phones here?

GORDON. Oh, yes. The only communication device God didn't invent was gossip, and that's the most advanced technology to date. It's what they call the music of the spheres – listen –

A cell phone ballet.
Beautiful music.
People moving through the rain
with umbrellas, talking into their cell phones,
fragments of lost conversations float up.
Jean listens.

Then, Mrs. Gottleib enters:

Of course he has my phone number, he's my son, I'm his mother. Who is this? Gordon?

Mrs. Gottleib exits.

JEAN. I heard her voice. On your phone. I thought – what can you tell a mother – about her dead son. I said: have a good day.

GORDON. Ah, mother.
She was never so comforting in life as she was in death. If mother did not approve, then mother did not appear to love. Funny. I never knew whether or not my own mother loved me.

JEAN. Oh, she loved you.
Your mother is beside herself with grief.

GORDON. No lies, Jean.

JEAN. No lies. Not that you deserve it.
Your mother said: I see it as my job to mourn him until the day I die.

GORDON. She did?

Jean nods.

How about that. My mother loved me after all.

Gordon's face, aglow from loving his mother best.

JEAN. Gordon – your face is different.

GORDON. How?

JEAN. You look well-loved.
Gordon?

GORDON. Mother?

Gordon disappears.
He is sucked into a cosmic pipeline

attached to his mother's hell.

JEAN. Gordon?
   Gordon!

A silence.

Jean, alone in the afterlife,
an Edward Hopper painting.

It's so quiet.
I'll just call Dwight.

Turn on. Turn on.
Stupid, stupid phone.

It won't go on.

I'll just pretend it's working.
Hello, Dwight, if you get this message, I am alone on
   my own planet
and I might be here for all time because I didn't tell
   you I love you
in the closet in the dark of the stationery store
because I got scared and then the phone rang
and when something rings you have to answer it.
Don't you?

STUPID STUPID PHONE!

She throws the phone down.
She bangs it on the ground until she destroys it.
It is the first time in a long time she has let herself cry.

Z.
Z!

She disappears.
Jean reappears on some lost luggage in the airport.
Dwight appears.

DWIGHT. Jean!

JEAN. Oh, Dwight! You have no idea what I've been through!

DWIGHT. Jean! I told you! You should never have gone off
   with those bad people! I forbidded you.

JEAN. You were right, Dwight! Dwight you were right! Did you get my message? I called you from my planet. It was so cold. Ad the air, oh it remembers, it all stays, like an Irish whistle they hear us. Did you hear me? Z!

DWIGHT. Oh, Jean!

JEAN. Can we go home? Do I have my kidneys? Does knowing someone help to love them best or does it all happen in one millisecond? I let your brother go. No phone. Oh, Dwight – call me darling.

She collapses in his arms.

DWIGHT. Oh, Jean, oh darling.

Scene Six

Dwight carries Jean to his mother's home.
Mrs. Gottlieb, holding a glass of bourbon.

DWIGHT. Mother! Jean passed out in Johannesburg.

Dwight tends to her.
Jean looks at Mrs. Gottlieb.

JEAN. Hello? Who are you? Put down your weapon!
Oh, Dwight!

DWIGHT. Here, have some bourbon, upsidown.

She does.

MRS. GOTTLIEB. A lot has happened since you've been
here, Jean. Dwight has been using his letter press to
publish books of subversive political theory and poetry
– haven't you, Dwight? He's on all the government
watch lists.

JEAN. But I've only been gone a day –

MRS. GOTTLIEB. No no Jean you've been gone months.

JEAN. That's not possible.

MRS. GOTTLIEB. Oh, yes. And Gordon's mistress – Carlotta
– she's taken over his business – yes – she got hold of
his old business contacts somehow and away she went.

Carlotta, in the distance, brandishing a phone.

JEAN. It was her!

MRS. GOTTLIEB. He left her nothing, you see, in the will –
and she'd been with him twelve years. Gordon should
have been more generous. And Hermia – well, Hermia
has had an offer to return to the stage.

JEAN. The stage?

MRS. GOTTLIEB. The ice follies. Hermia used to be a world
class dramatic skater, but Gordon thought it was undig-
nified for his wife to dance on the ice wearing loud
make-up. So she left the follies for him. Let that be a
lesson to you, Jean. Never leave off follies for a man.
Well, now the follies have her back. She's on tour. Den-
mark, then San Jose.

Hermia, in the distance, ice dancing.
Dramatic skating music.

MRS. GOTTLIEB. And I for one am happy for her. Everyone's moved on. Except for me.

He was my only son. That is to say – he was my first
son. The first sometimes feels like the only – you must
know that from your own sexual experiences, or are
you a virgin Jean?

DWIGHT. Mother! What would make you feel better, Jean?

MRS. GOTTLIEB. A cold compress, a quiche?

JEAN. I think I'd like a steak actually.

MRS. GOTTLIEB. A steak? I thought you didn't eat meat.

JEAN. I'm starving.

MRS. GOTTLIEB. Carmen! PUT A STEAK ON THE FIRE!
Rare?

JEAN. Yes!

MRS. GOTTLIEB. RARE!

You know, I've tried to call Gordon but his voice is no
longer on the out-going message. I call his old number,
and no voice. And somehow – now – I feel he's truly
dead.

JEAN. I have something to tell you, Mrs. Gottlieb.

MRS. GOTTLIEB. Well then don't stand on ceremony, dear.

JEAN. Gordon's gone up the pipeline to spend eternity on
your planet since it seems you loved him most.

MRS. GOTTLIEB. What?

JEAN. It's hard to explain. You won't understand until you
die.

MRS. GOTTLIEB. You've seen Gordon?

JEAN. Oh, yes.

MRS. GOTTLIEB. That's where you've been?

JEAN. Yes.

MRS. GOTTLIEB. And he's waiting for me there? In heaven?

JEAN. It's a kind of heaven, I guess. There are these – laundromats.

DWIGHT. Laundromats?

MRS. GOTTLIEB. Does he have to do his own laundry?

JEAN. Yes he has to do it himself now.

MRS. GOTTLIEB. Is he punished?

JEAN. Not really. Now he's with you. Or – he's waiting for you.

MRS. GOTTLIEB. For me alone?

JEAN. Yes.

MRS. GOTTLIEB. He has no one else to console him?

JEAN. No.

MRS. GOTTLIEB. Gordon! Gordon, I'm coming!
     Together we'll play all the games we played when you were little. Hush, little wormy, on my arm, we'll get a spider to calm you down! Gordon, wait for your mother! It won't be long now!

JEAN. Wait, don't!

> **MRS. GOTTLIEB** *walks off stage with determination.*
> *She might sing a reprise of "You'll never walk alone."*
> *Off stage she throws herself into the flames with the steak*
> *and self immolates but we don't need to hear or see that.*

JEAN. The fire – the steak on the fire – oh no – the pit –
     it's such a large barbeque in the backyard –
     Aren't you going to stop her?

DWIGHT. No. They'll be happy together.
     She always did love him best.

JEAN. So that's that?

DWIGHT. Good-bye mother. Kiss my brother for me and be happy.

JEAN. Oh, Dwight.
     I want to make sure we get on the same
     planet when we die.
     I don't want to end up with my garden
     or my dog for all time.
     Let's start loving each other right now, Dwight –
     not a mediocre love, but the strongest love in the world, absolutely requited.

So that we know and all the omniscient things of heaven know too – let's love each other absolutely.

DWIGHT. Then let's do it, Jean. Let's love each other better than the worthies did.

JEAN. Who are the worthies?

DWIGHT. It's from a poem.

JEAN. Did you write it?

DWIGHT. No John Donne did. I'll take you to my letter press and show you.

JEAN. Now?

DWIGHT. Not right now.

Now we kiss. And the lights go out.

They kiss,
and the lights go out.
The end.

NOTES FOR THE DIRECTOR AND DESIGNERS:

On the cell phone ballet...

I kept a record of conversations I overheard on cell phones as I was writing this play to use as found text in the cell phone ballet. The notion was that fragments from the ruin float up and meet Jean – and that they are almost beautiful. The problem is that when you record found text with actor's voices, it no longer feels authentic, because the voice itself is not found. You might then consider going round and recording people's overheard cell phone conversations. Or use messages that have already been left on your phone. If you choose to use my own text to layer over the music of the spheres, here are the most useful found bits of text that I've incorporated into different productions:

> I'm disappointed in you – I thought you could stay on – there was more than a million dollars involved – I talked to Jack – in human resources –

> You have to sign the death certificate at the top and at the bottom – that's all –

> I love you

> Yes, Dr. Stevens, thank you I can come in then for the biopsy – or should we make it later? Eleven?

> Do you know how it hurts when you pick up the phone in that tone of voice?

> I love you.

> Good-bye

You might consider layering these bits into a song, or spoken over a song, having them vaguely sung, or not, having non-actors record them, finding bits of your own found text, or translating some or all of it into Japanese and various other languages. And if all else fails, cut the cell phone ballet and keep the repeated voices of Jean and Mrs. Gottlieb. It rankles me to be this vague, but the cell phone ballet depends so much on the sound designer, director, and all the rest of it. As for choreography, there might be a simple pas de deux while people are on their cell phones, or the movement might be as simple as people walking through the rain carrying umbrellas while talking on cell phone. One thing I learned is that if the movement is complex, the music and voices should be simple; if the voices are complex, the movement should be simple. I wish I could tell you there is one definitive way to crack this oyster but it's up to your collective imagination. the movement should be simple. I wish I could tell you there is one definitive way to crack this oyster but it's up to your collective imagination.

On double casting:

If you do choose to double-cast Dwight and Gordon, you'll have to cut the last stage direction about Gordon entering at the end of the first act. And you might consider changing the following stage direction:

Jean stares at Dwight. He looks so much like Gordon. But Jean doesn't want to remind anyone of Gordon's death, so she doesn't comment on the resemblance.

to a line of dialogue:

JEAN: You look so much like him.

And if you choose to double cast Hermia and the Other Woman, cut Carlotta's entrance in the background before Hermia enters skating. I would also imagine that Hermia would have a blonde wig and Carlotta would have a brunette wig.

On the moments of song:

If you do choose to sing "You'll Never Walk Alone" you'll need to contact the estate of Rodgers and Hammerstein for permission. Mrs. Gottlieb might sing only a fragment,

or she might sing the whole song.

As for the Edward Hopper moments...

I think they are about finding one simple gesture – Jean looks towards a window – and suspends – and the lights imperceptibly shift. They are about the solitary figure inside the landscape or architecture. They are about being alone inside of or in relation to the modern.

As for everything else...

There is a great deal of silence and empty space in this play, but the pauses should not be epic.

There might be an extended fight sequence in the airport in Johannesburg.

I call Jean's stories confabulations, I never call them lies...

The paper houses that fall on Jean and Dwight at the end of Part One should ideally be made of high quality or hand made paper. Go to a paper store and touch the paper.

Transitions are fluid. Space is fluid. There is not a lot of stuff on the stage.

Enjoy yourself.